D0493419

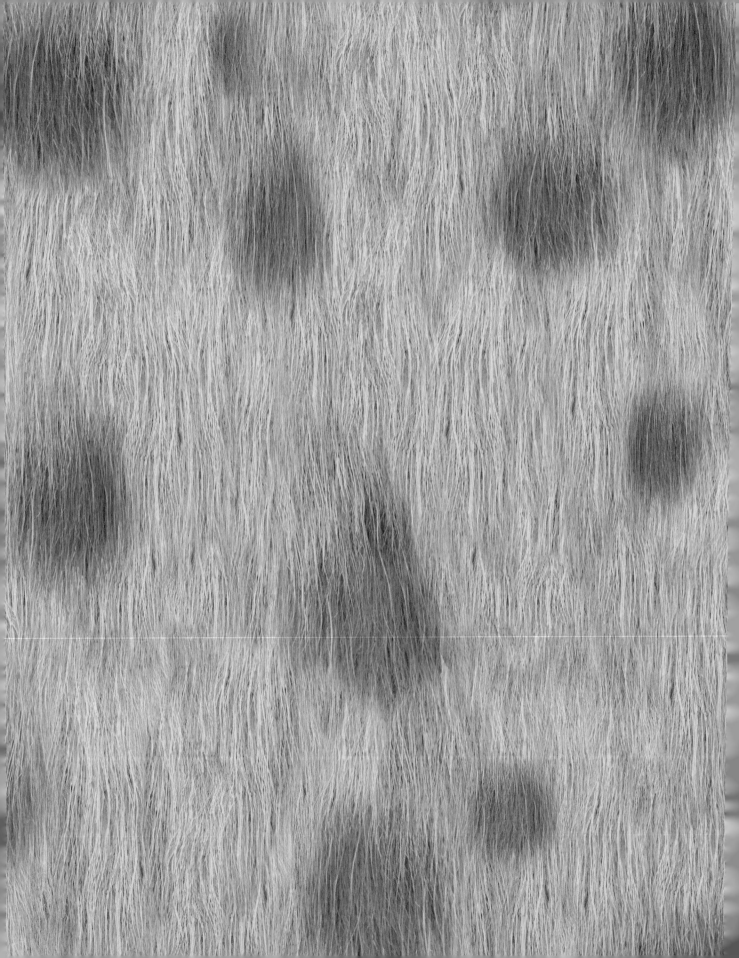

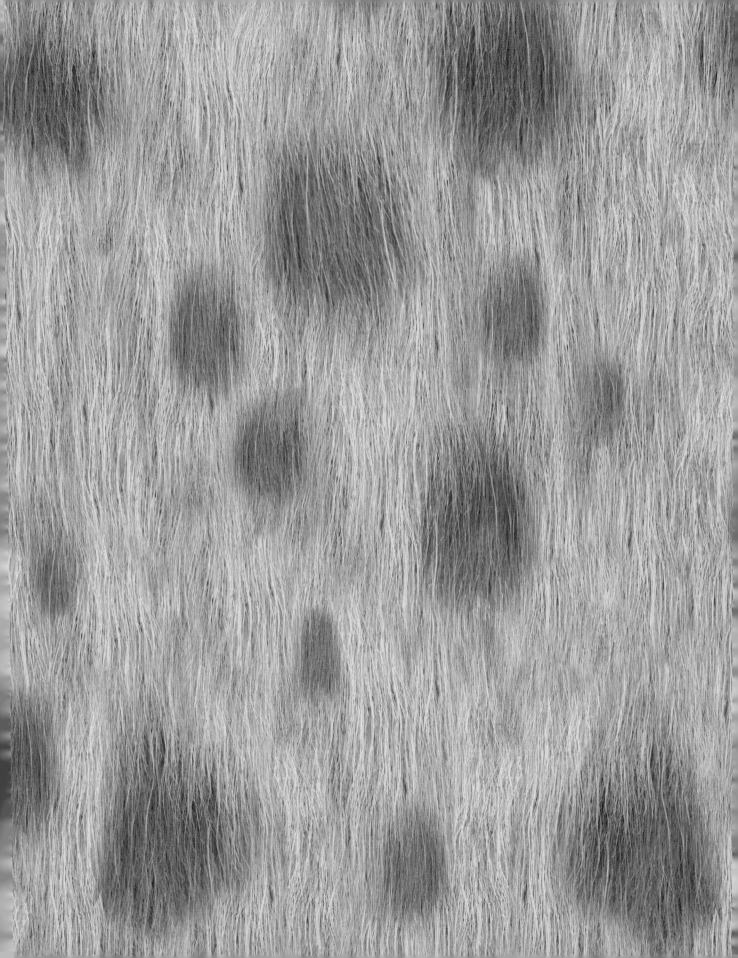

Published by Ladybird Books Ltd.,
80 Strand, London WC2R ORL
A Penguin Company

LADYBIRD and the device of a ladybird are trademarks of Ladybird Books Ltd.

Copyright © 2001 Disney Enterprises, Inc./Pixar Animation Studios

*All rights reserved. No part of this publication may be reproduced,
stored in a retrieval system, or transmitted in any form or by any means,
electronic, mechanical, photocopying, recording or otherwise,
without the prior consent of the copyright owner.*

Printed in UK.

www.ladybird.co.uk

DISNEY·PIXAR
MONSTERS, INC.

Ladybird

Moonlight stole into the room, into the darkest corners. It slid silently across the bed, where a small boy lay sleeping. All was silent.

The curtains fluttered gently in the breeze, and a wardrobe door creaked faintly.

The boy awoke.

In the shadows, a pair of gleaming eyes watched and waited.

The boy peered from under his covers.

Suddenly a huge and frightening monster crashed, roaring, from the wardrobe.

The boy began to scream. And the monster screamed back!

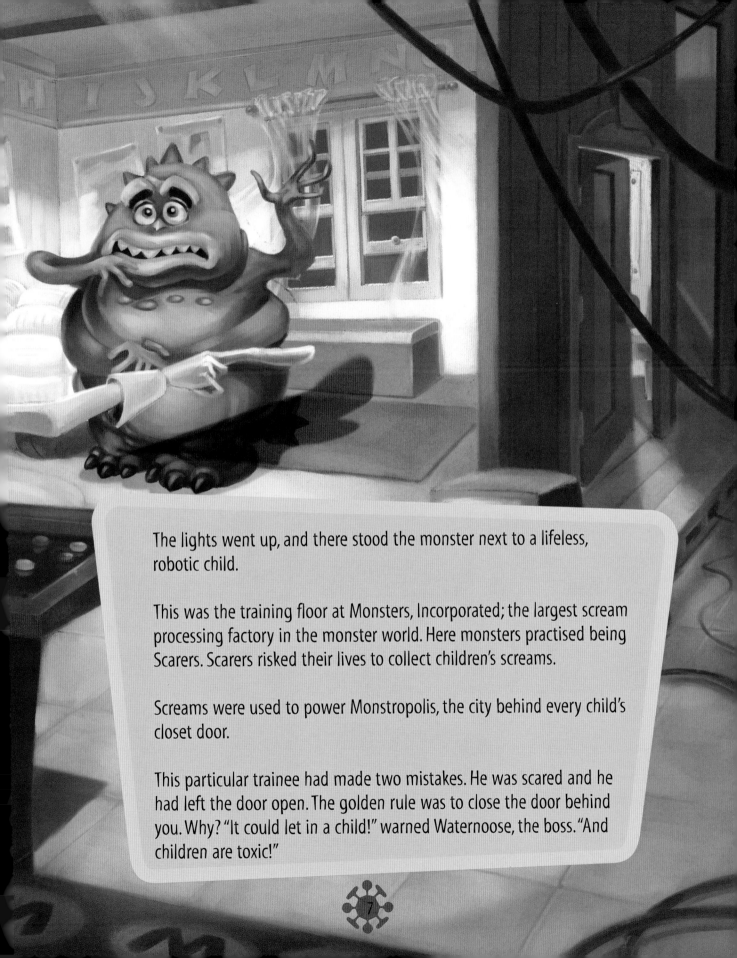

The lights went up, and there stood the monster next to a lifeless, robotic child.

This was the training floor at Monsters, Incorporated; the largest scream processing factory in the monster world. Here monsters practised being Scarers. Scarers risked their lives to collect children's screams.

Screams were used to power Monstropolis, the city behind every child's closet door.

This particular trainee had made two mistakes. He was scared and he had left the door open. The golden rule was to close the door behind you. Why? "It could let in a child!" warned Waternoose, the boss. "And children are toxic!"

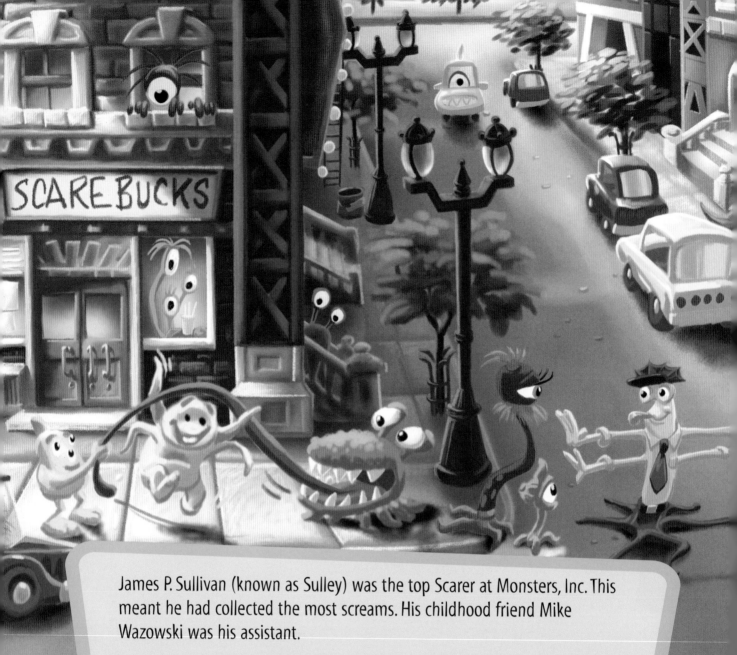

James P. Sullivan (known as Sulley) was the top Scarer at Monsters, Inc. This meant he had collected the most screams. His childhood friend Mike Wazowski was his assistant.

Across town, Mike and Sulley were excitedly watching the new Monsters, Inc. commercial on TV. They were in it! It explained that although MI had the best Scarers around, it was getting more and more difficult to do a good job – kids were just not so easy to scare any more. Without screams, which provided power to the monster world, the lights in Monstropolis would all go out.

Mike and Sulley walked to work that day because of the scream crisis.

8

The Monsters, Inc. lobby was alive with monsters hurrying to and fro. Celia, the receptionist, soon spotted Mike, and the snakes framing her pretty face turned to greet him.

"Oh, Schmoopsie-Poo . . . happy birthday!" said Mike. "I've booked us a table at a little place called Harryhausen's! See you at 5.01, and not a minute later."

"Oh, Googley-Woogley, you remembered," smiled Celia and her snakes.

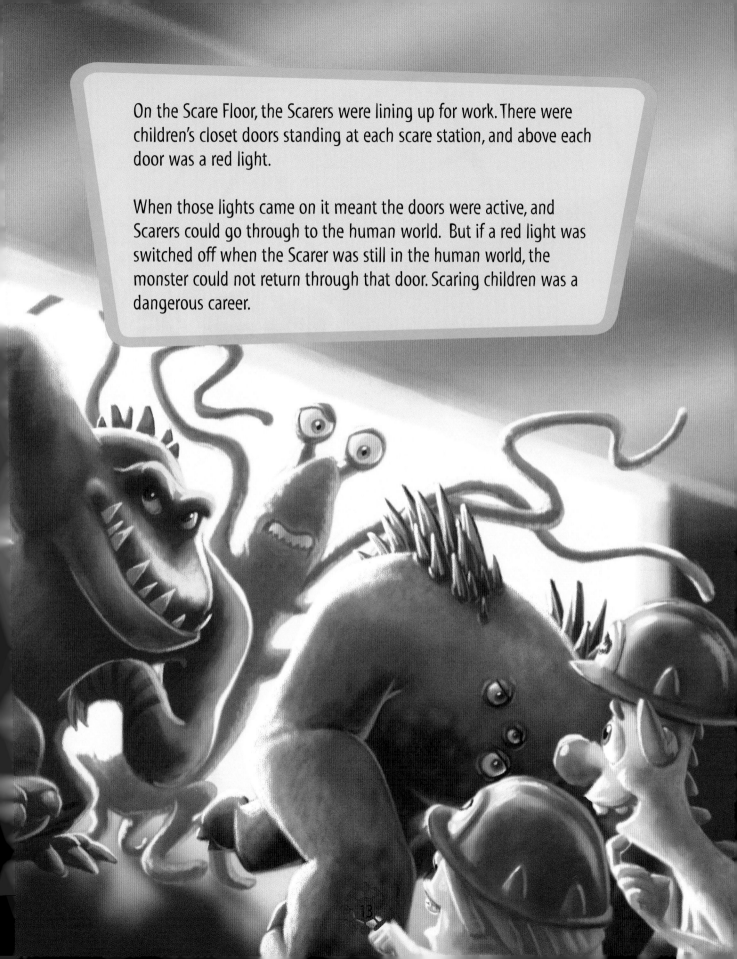

On the Scare Floor, the Scarers were lining up for work. There were children's closet doors standing at each scare station, and above each door was a red light.

When those lights came on it meant the doors were active, and Scarers could go through to the human world. But if a red light was switched off when the Scarer was still in the human world, the monster could not return through that door. Scaring children was a dangerous career.

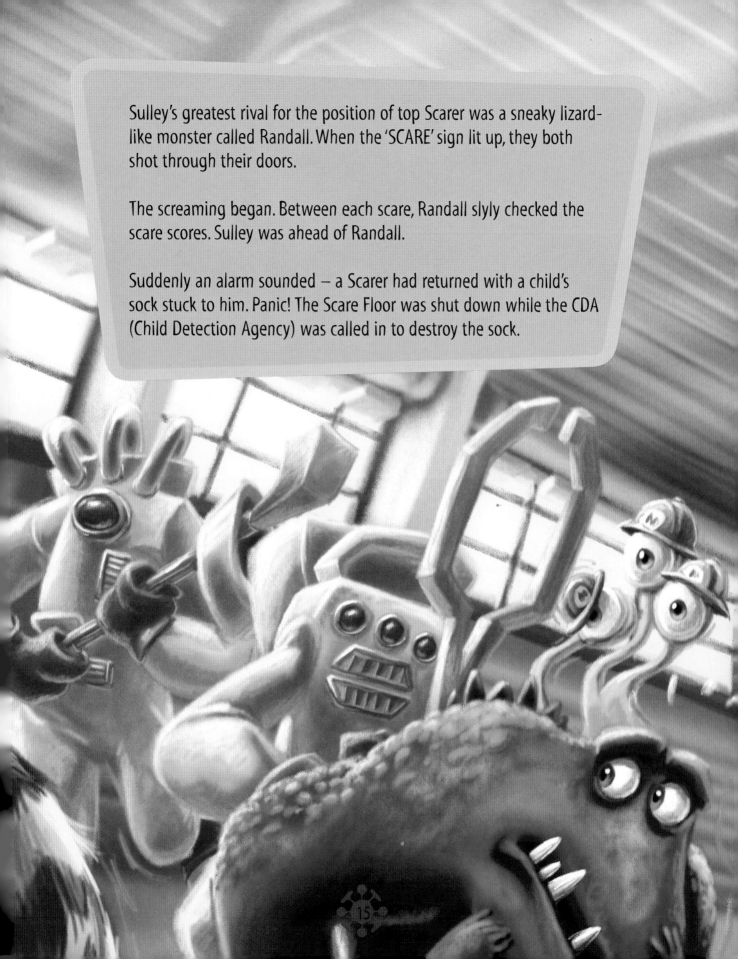

Sulley's greatest rival for the position of top Scarer was a sneaky lizard-like monster called Randall. When the 'SCARE' sign lit up, they both shot through their doors.

The screaming began. Between each scare, Randall slyly checked the scare scores. Sulley was ahead of Randall.

Suddenly an alarm sounded — a Scarer had returned with a child's sock stuck to him. Panic! The Scare Floor was shut down while the CDA (Child Detection Agency) was called in to destroy the sock.

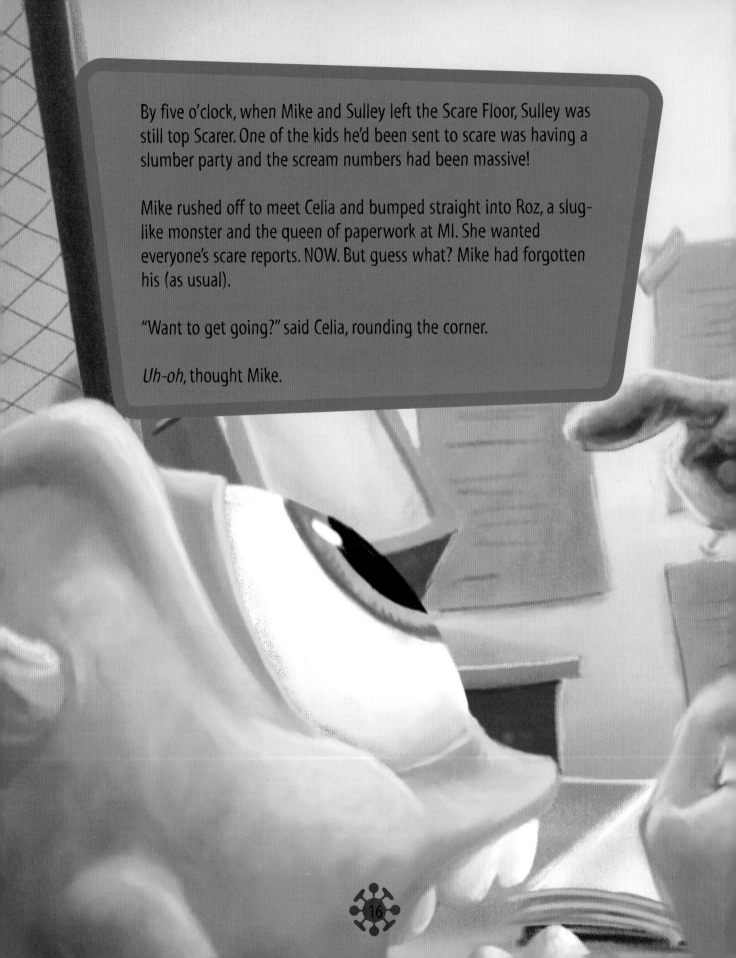

By five o'clock, when Mike and Sulley left the Scare Floor, Sulley was still top Scarer. One of the kids he'd been sent to scare was having a slumber party and the scream numbers had been massive!

Mike rushed off to meet Celia and bumped straight into Roz, a slug-like monster and the queen of paperwork at MI. She wanted everyone's scare reports. NOW. But guess what? Mike had forgotten his (as usual).

"Want to get going?" said Celia, rounding the corner.

Uh-oh, thought Mike.

Seeing his friend in trouble, Sulley quickly offered to go back for the reports himself.

Mike and Celia went off happily, and Sulley wandered back to the Scare Floor.

A door stood in the middle of the empty room. Its light was on, showing it to be active. Maybe someone was working late, thought Sulley. He pushed it open.

"Psst . . . anyone scaring in there?" There was no answer.

Shrugging, he closed the door and turned to see — to his surprise — a little girl, holding his tail and giggling . . .

"Kitty!" she laughed. He was so furry!

Sulley was terrified. Children were toxic! What had he done? He pushed her back through the door, but she popped out again!

In a panic, Sulley ran to the locker room, put the little girl into a sports bag, and crept back to the Scare Floor.

But someone else was there too. Sulley could feel it. He glanced around and saw Randall. He was sending the child's door back to the vaults.

Now what?

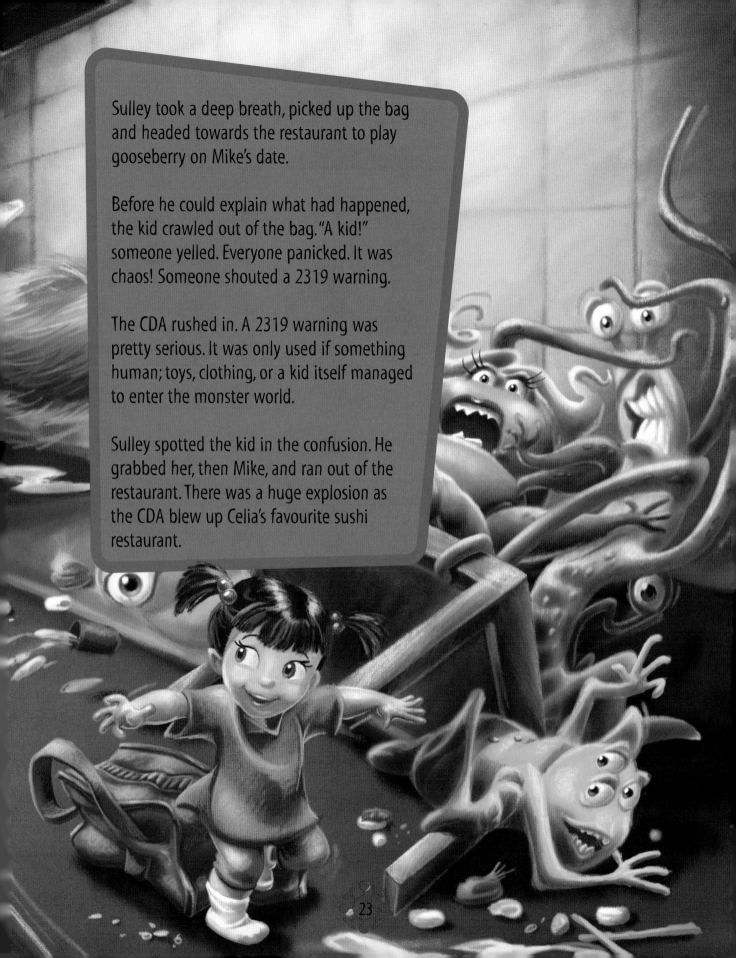

Sulley took a deep breath, picked up the bag and headed towards the restaurant to play gooseberry on Mike's date.

Before he could explain what had happened, the kid crawled out of the bag. "A kid!" someone yelled. Everyone panicked. It was chaos! Someone shouted a 2319 warning.

The CDA rushed in. A 2319 warning was pretty serious. It was only used if something human; toys, clothing, or a kid itself managed to enter the monster world.

Sulley spotted the kid in the confusion. He grabbed her, then Mike, and ran out of the restaurant. There was a huge explosion as the CDA blew up Celia's favourite sushi restaurant.

Back home, the friends watched the child. Mike was furious with Sulley, as well as terrified.

The girl soon found Mike's teddy bear — all one-eyed monsters have one-eyed teddy bears. Mike tried to grab it back and lost his balance. She laughed — he looked so funny! Suddenly the lights grew brighter and then blew out. Sulley looked up, puzzled.

Later, Sulley said, "I'm sure the kid's not dangerous. What if we just put her back in her door?"

"Whaaat??" screamed Mike.

The next day, Mike and Sulley marched straight into Monsters, Inc. They also marched straight into the boss! They had disguised the child as a baby monster and Sulley managed to persuade Mr Waternoose that she was a relative. Poor Mike's heart was thumping.

They hurried on. Mike left Sulley and the kid in the locker room while he raced off to find the keycard for her door. Now they'd got this far, he just wanted to get her back where she belonged – and soon!

When Mike returned, the three of them casually wandered onto the Scare Floor.

They stood at their station and Mike swiped the keycard into the control panel. The machinery of the door vault powered up and a door plonked down. Sulley peered at it.

"Mike," he whispered through gritted teeth. "This isn't Boo's door."

His friend was horrified — but not because of the door.

"Sulley, you can't name it! Say goodbye to . . ." He looked round for Boo. But while they'd been arguing, she had disappeared.

It was panic time again as they looked around frantically.

Uh-oh. There was Celia. She was furious about her ruined dinner and told Mike so – loudly.

Randall was slithering down the corridor, heard them arguing, and glanced at the picture of the remains of the sushi restaurant on the front of his newspaper. He put two and two together and suspected Mike had the girl.

Randall's evil face grinned as he hatched a plan.

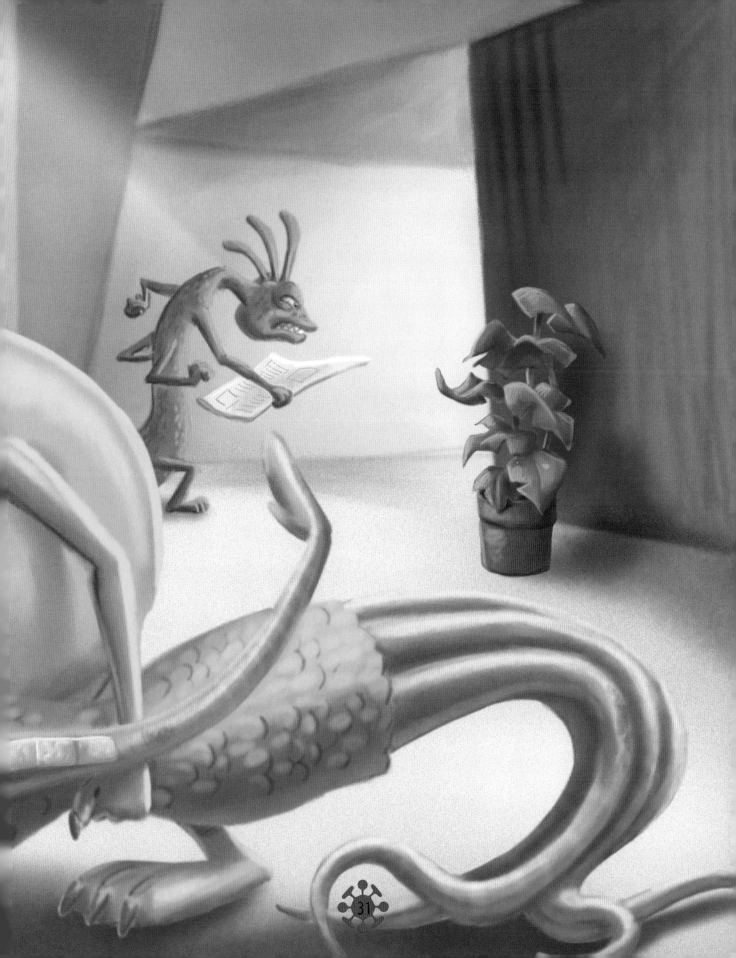

When Mike escaped from Celia, he ran to catch up with Sulley.
But rounding a corner, he bumped into Randall.

"It's here in the factory, isn't it?" said the lizard monster menacingly.

"You're not pinning this on me." Mike was sweating now.

"I know how to make this go away," winked Randall. Mike stopped
breathing. "The kid's door will be at my station at lunchtime. The Scare
Floor will be empty, so you can put it back."

Mike stared at him, horrified,
with his big green
mouth open.

When he had calmed down, Mike found Sulley, who was in a terrible state — he couldn't find Boo anywhere.

But Boo was quite happy. Eventually they found her charging around with the kids in the creche. Suddenly, one of the little ones bit Mike!

"Owwww!"

Boo laughed. The lights grew brighter.

As Mike, Sulley, and Boo rushed to the empty Scare Floor, Mike hurriedly explained Randall's plan.

There it was. Boo's door. Just as Randall had promised.

But Sulley didn't trust Randall.

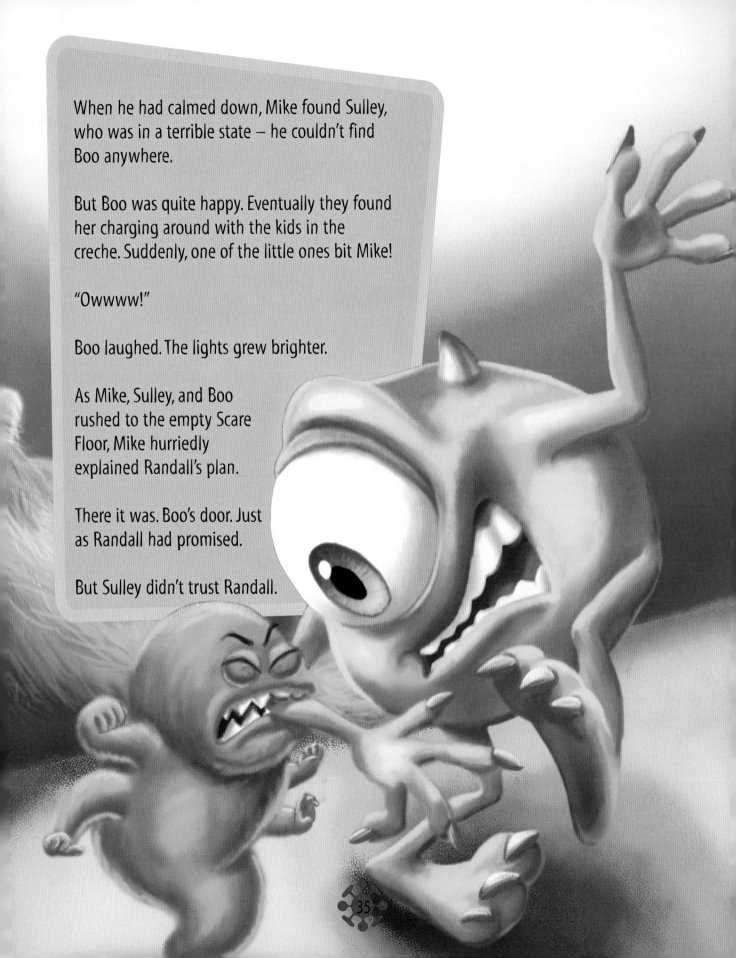

To prove it was safe, Mike jumped through the door himself – and right into a trap.

A box was lowered over him. Sulley hid and watched, horrified, as Randall slammed it shut, walked back through the door and off the Scare Floor, thinking he'd got Boo.

Sulley followed Randall down the corridor until, suddenly, a secret door opened. Randall stepped through. Sulley followed. Around a corner, he was shocked to see a huge scream extracting machine which Randall was obviously hoping to use on Boo.

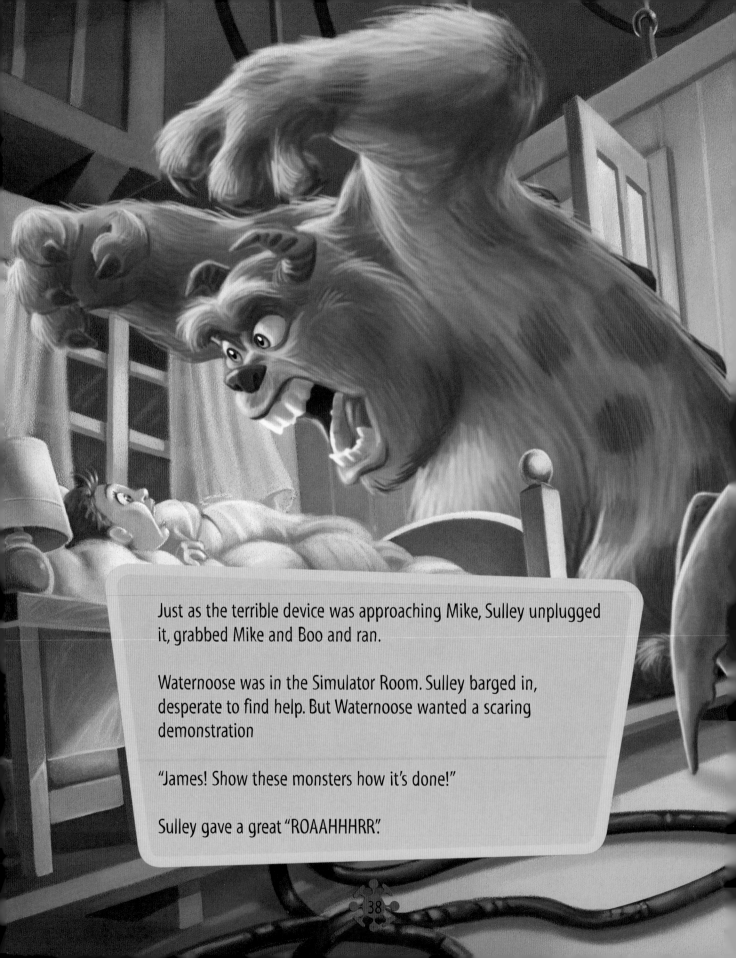

Just as the terrible device was approaching Mike, Sulley unplugged it, grabbed Mike and Boo and ran.

Waternoose was in the Simulator Room. Sulley barged in, desperate to find help. But Waternoose wanted a scaring demonstration

"James! Show these monsters how it's done!"

Sulley gave a great "ROAAHHHRR".

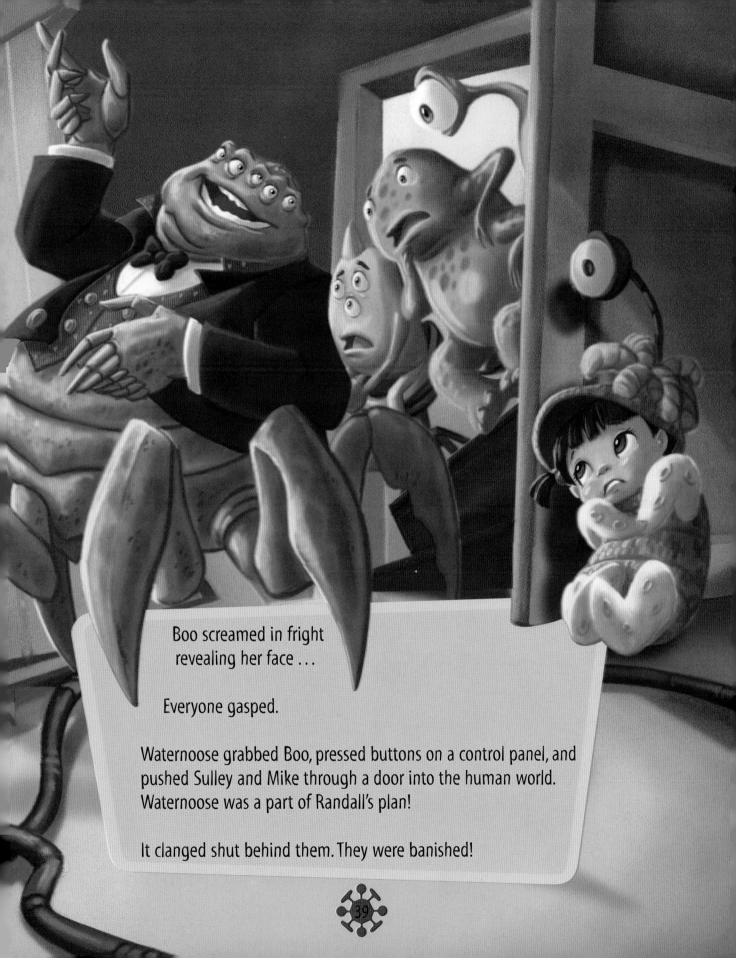

Boo screamed in fright
revealing her face . . .

Everyone gasped.

Waternoose grabbed Boo, pressed buttons on a control panel, and pushed Sulley and Mike through a door into the human world. Waternoose was a part of Randall's plan!

It clanged shut behind them. They were banished!

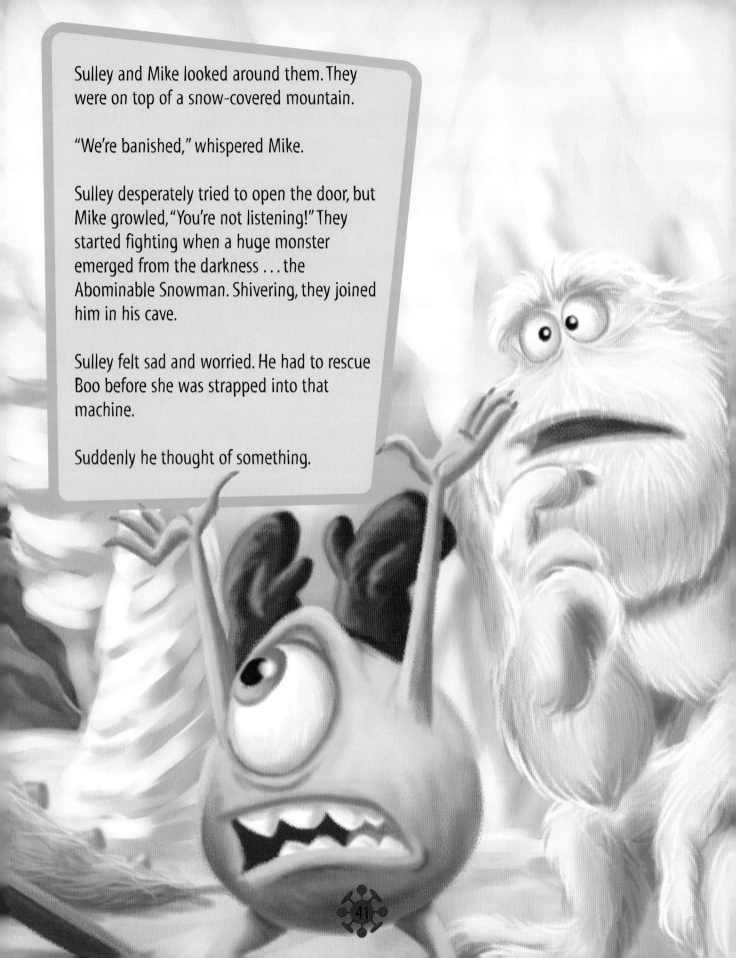

Sulley and Mike looked around them. They were on top of a snow-covered mountain.

"We're banished," whispered Mike.

Sulley desperately tried to open the door, but Mike growled, "You're not listening!" They started fighting when a huge monster emerged from the darkness ... the Abominable Snowman. Shivering, they joined him in his cave.

Sulley felt sad and worried. He had to rescue Boo before she was strapped into that machine.

Suddenly he thought of something.

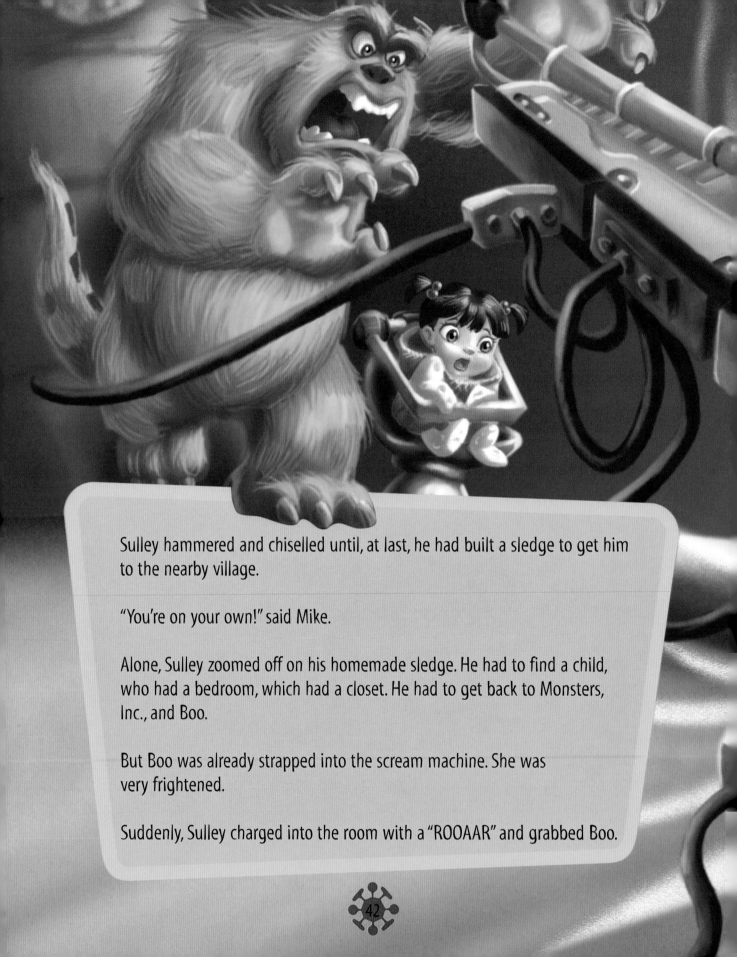

Sulley hammered and chiselled until, at last, he had built a sledge to get him to the nearby village.

"You're on your own!" said Mike.

Alone, Sulley zoomed off on his homemade sledge. He had to find a child, who had a bedroom, which had a closet. He had to get back to Monsters, Inc., and Boo.

But Boo was already strapped into the scream machine. She was very frightened.

Suddenly, Sulley charged into the room with a "ROOAAR" and grabbed Boo.

42

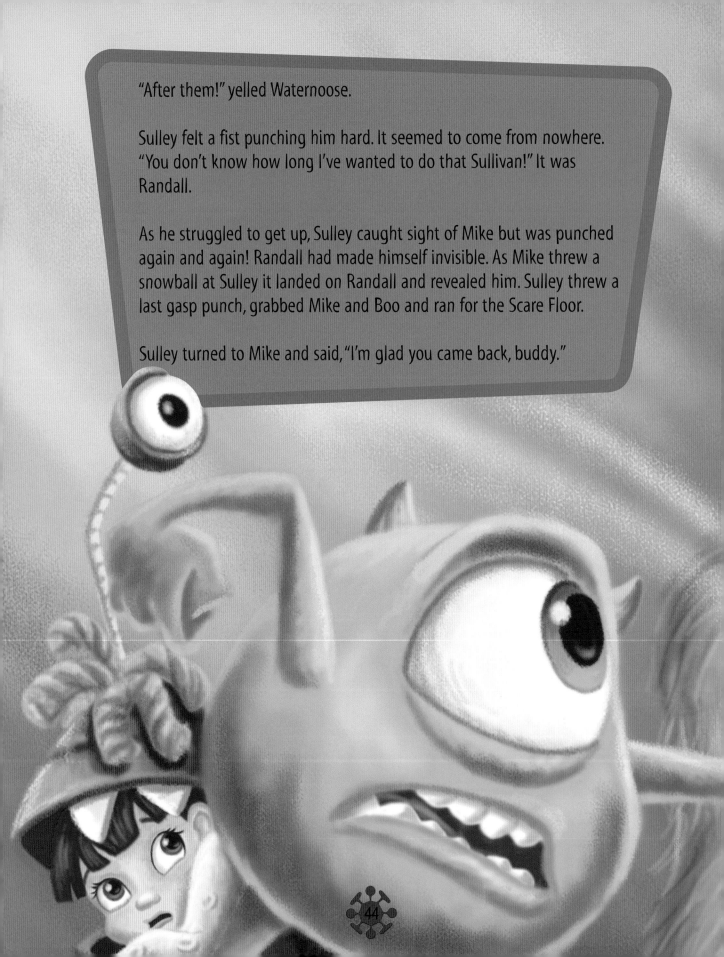

"After them!" yelled Waternoose.

Sulley felt a fist punching him hard. It seemed to come from nowhere. "You don't know how long I've wanted to do that Sullivan!" It was Randall.

As he struggled to get up, Sulley caught sight of Mike but was punched again and again! Randall had made himself invisible. As Mike threw a snowball at Sulley it landed on Randall and revealed him. Sulley threw a last gasp punch, grabbed Mike and Boo and ran for the Scare Floor.

Sulley turned to Mike and said, "I'm glad you came back, buddy."

Then Celia got in on the act. She grabbed Mike.

"Shmoopsie-Poo!" he puffed. "I really can't talk."

"Michael, if you don't tell me what's going on, we're over!" she screamed.

Mike gave in. "OK. That kid they're looking for – Sulley let her in and now Randall's after us."

"You expect me to believe that!" she huffed. Then she caught sight of Boo, gasped, and let go of Mike.

"I love you, Shmoopsie-Poo!" he called desperately, as Sulley pulled him along.

At last, they were on the
Scare Floor. Mike swiped their card. They saw Boo's door in the distance
on the way into the vault. Randall was right behind them now. There
was no time to waste.

"OK," said Sulley. "We're going to have to do this the hard way." He
rushed to the nearest Door Station and, clutching Boo, grabbed onto a
door heading back to the vaults. Mike just managed to grab onto
Sulley's tail as he disappeared.

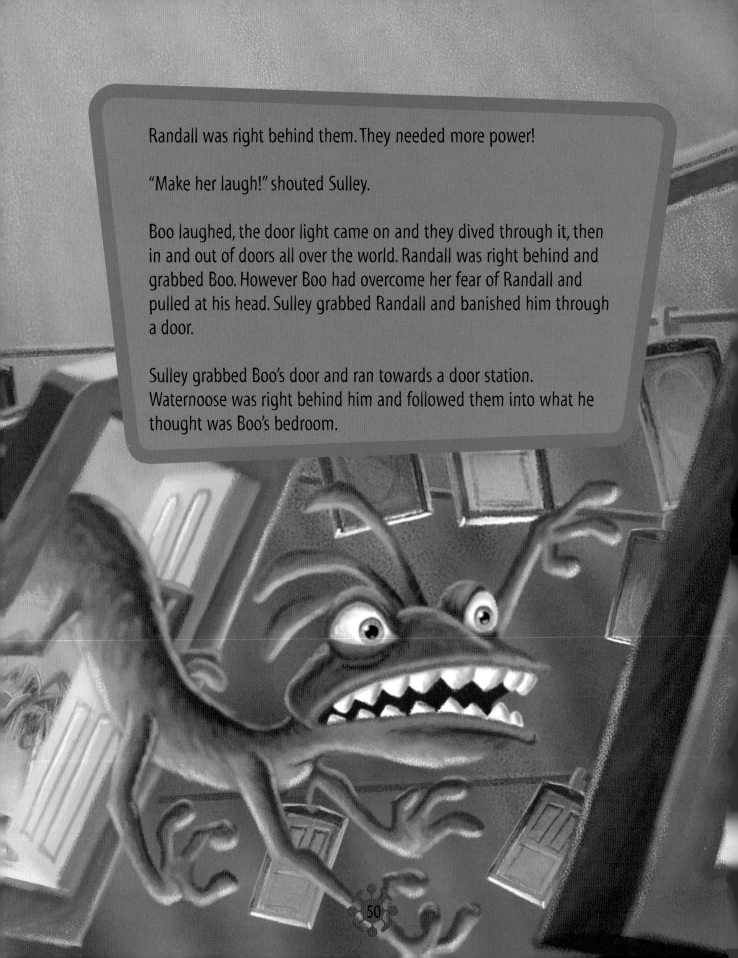

Randall was right behind them. They needed more power!

"Make her laugh!" shouted Sulley.

Boo laughed, the door light came on and they dived through it, then in and out of doors all over the world. Randall was right behind and grabbed Boo. However Boo had overcome her fear of Randall and pulled at his head. Sulley grabbed Randall and banished him through a door.

Sulley grabbed Boo's door and ran towards a door station. Waternoose was right behind him and followed them into what he thought was Boo's bedroom.

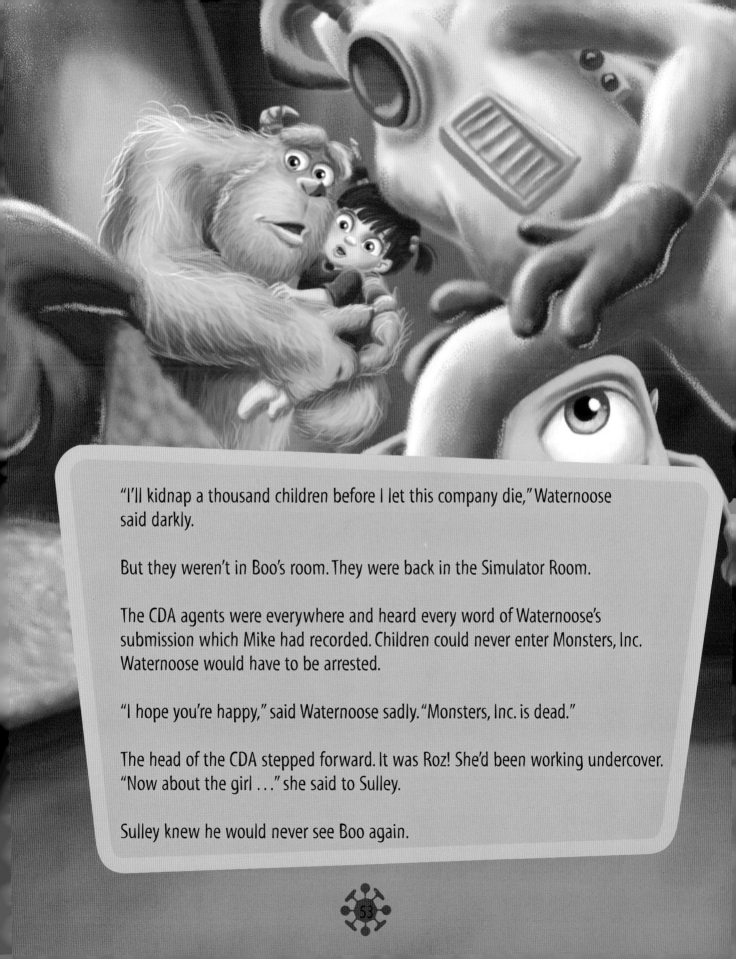

"I'll kidnap a thousand children before I let this company die," Waternoose
said darkly.

But they weren't in Boo's room. They were back in the Simulator Room.

The CDA agents were everywhere and heard every word of Waternoose's
submission which Mike had recorded. Children could never enter Monsters, Inc.
Waternoose would have to be arrested.

"I hope you're happy," said Waternoose sadly. "Monsters, Inc. is dead."

The head of the CDA stepped forward. It was Roz! She'd been working undercover.
"Now about the girl . . ." she said to Sulley.

Sulley knew he would never see Boo again.

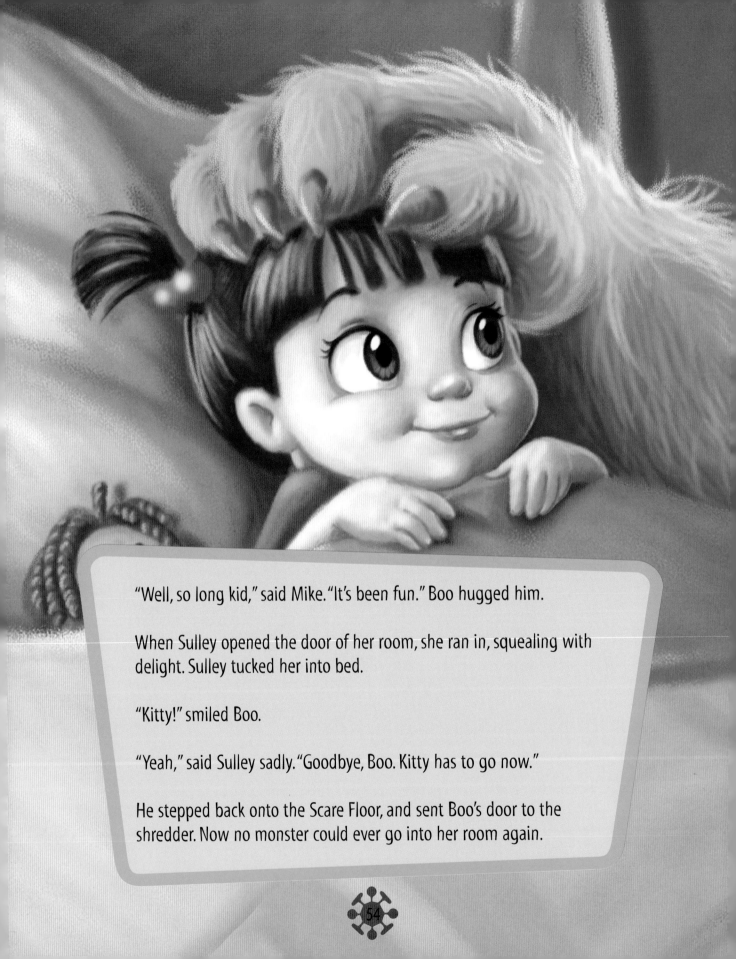

"Well, so long kid," said Mike. "It's been fun." Boo hugged him.

When Sulley opened the door of her room, she ran in, squealing with delight. Sulley tucked her into bed.

"Kitty!" smiled Boo.

"Yeah," said Sulley sadly. "Goodbye, Boo. Kitty has to go now."

He stepped back onto the Scare Floor, and sent Boo's door to the shredder. Now no monster could ever go into her room again.

Sulley had lost Boo, but life wasn't too bad. Since the discovery that laughter created more power than screams, there had been a Laugh Floor at Monsters, Inc. and Sulley was now in charge.

These days, monsters made children scream with laughter, not fear. They threw custard pies, slipped on banana skins, and told jokes. That all meant power for Monstropolis.

Mike and Celia were together again. But Mike knew Sulley missed Boo, and he had a plan . . .

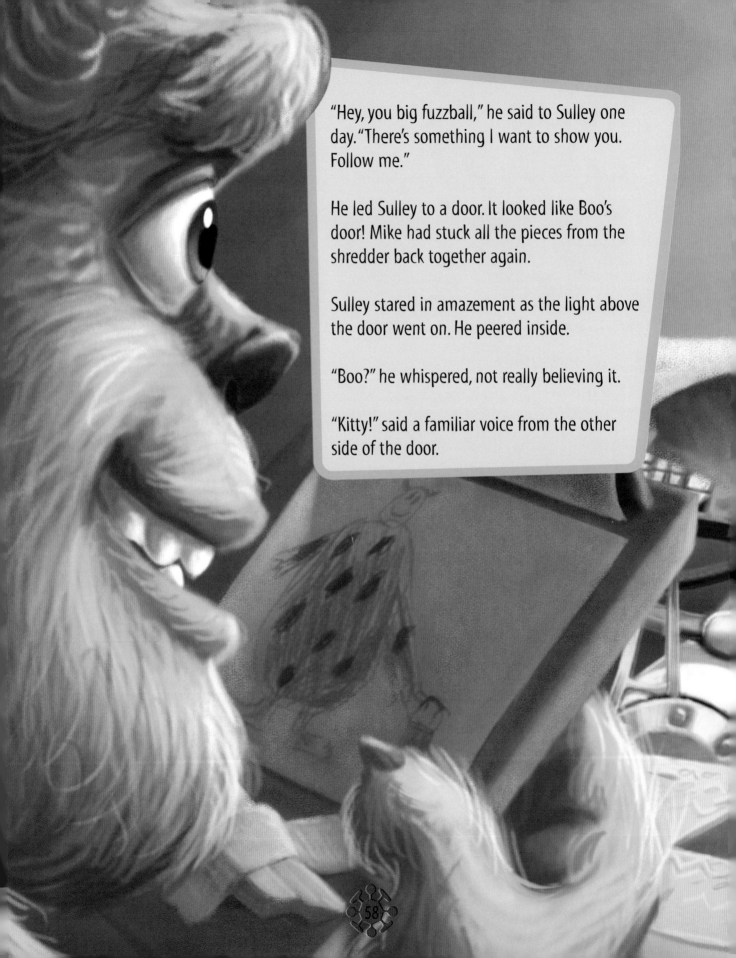

"Hey, you big fuzzball," he said to Sulley one day. "There's something I want to show you. Follow me."

He led Sulley to a door. It looked like Boo's door! Mike had stuck all the pieces from the shredder back together again.

Sulley stared in amazement as the light above the door went on. He peered inside.

"Boo?" he whispered, not really believing it.

"Kitty!" said a familiar voice from the other side of the door.

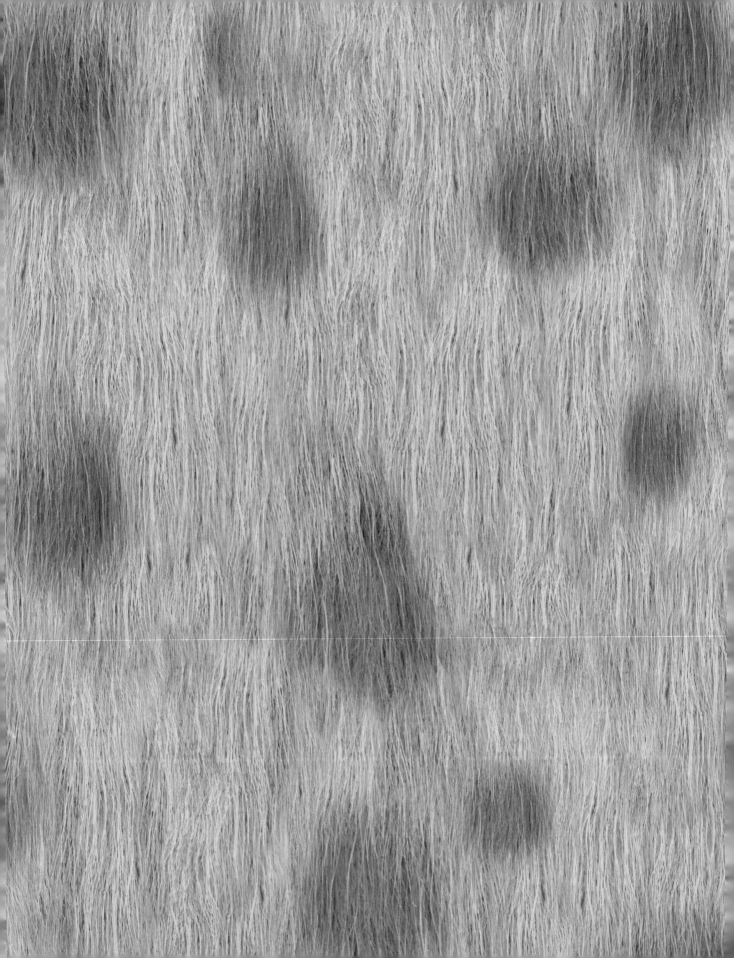

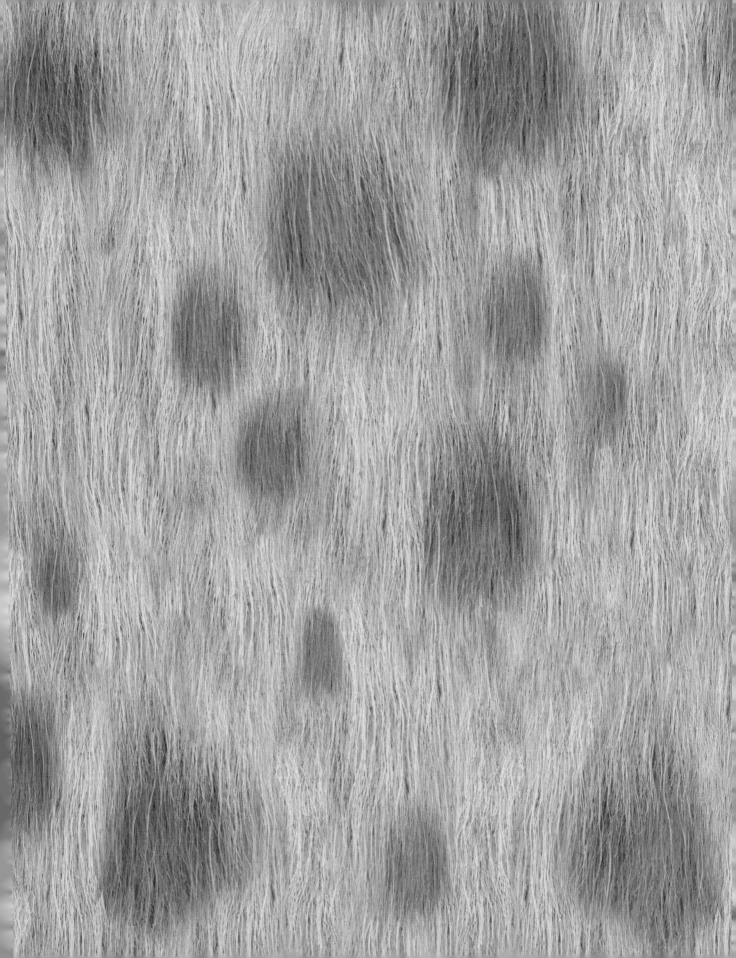